P9-CPZ-868

Text and illustrations copyright © 2018 by Matt James
Published in Canada and the USA in 2018 by Groundwood Books

Groundwood Books / House of Anansi Press
groundwoodbooks.com

We acknowledge for their financial support of our publishing program the Canada Council for the Arts, the Ontario Arts Council and the Government of Canada.

For Sheila Barry.
With thanks to Julius, Noble, Niamh and Madeleine.

Canada Council   Conseil des Arts
for the Arts   du Canada

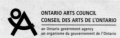

ONTARIO ARTS COUNCIL
CONSEIL DES ARTS DE L'ONTARIO
an Ontario government agency
un organisme du gouvernement de l'Ontario

With the participation of the Government of Canada
Avec la participation du gouvernement du Canada | Canadä

RECEIVED
JUL 1 8 2018

Library and Archives Canada Cataloguing in Publication
James, Matt, author, illustrator
The funeral / [written and illustrated by] Matt James.
Issued in print and electronic formats.
ISBN 978-1-55498-908-9 (hardcover). —
ISBN 978-1-55498-909-6 (PDF)
I. Title.
PS8619.A6357F86 2018   jC813'.6   C2017-905232-2
C2017-905233-0

The art was done in acrylic and ink on masonite. The dimensional elements were made from cut paper, masking tape, rolled-up twine, cardboard and scroll-sawn masonite, all painted with acrylic. A few pieces were processed digitally. The background illustration on pages 8-9 was adapted from Vecteezy.com.
Design by Michael Solomon
Printed and bound in Malaysia

FSC
www.fsc.org

MIX
Paper from
responsible sources
FSC® C012700

The FUNERAL
– Matt James

ⓖ GROUNDWOOD BOOKS   HOUSE OF ANANSI PRESS   TORONTO   BERKELEY

"No school for Norma!" said Norma, putting on her mother's shoe.

A few days earlier, there had been a phone call.
Her great-uncle Frank had died, and today was
for saying goodbye.

Norma was practicing her sad face in the mirror of her parents' room. Though she was, in fact, pretty happy.

It was a day off from school, and she would be spending it with her cousin Ray. Her FAVORITE cousin, Ray.

There was a little flag on the car that drove them to the church. Norma tried to sound out the word printed on it.

"F—U—N," she said.

And then she said it again.

The big black cars moved slowly through town.

Norma rolled her window down. Then she rolled it up again. Up, down, up, down, up, down, until her dad pressed the button that took her window privileges away.

In the parking lot, her mother put a million kleenexes in her purse and checked her makeup.

"Norma!"
She heard Ray from across the parking lot.
"Norma, Norma."

The funeral was about to begin,
and into the church they went.

As he took his seat in the row ahead,
Ray passed Norma his giraffe. It was wet with
slobber.

"Gross," she whispered to Ray, who didn't hear her.

Norma loved her mother's purse. She put her face right into it and breathed deeply, the smell a mix of toothpaste and makeup and sweet warm leather — different from the old book smell of the church.

Norma liked the feeling she got sitting there, as invisible dust appeared and was trapped, dancing in beams of light.

And oh, how looong they sat on those
hard seats, with all that talk about God
and souls, and not very much talk about
Uncle Frank.

Ray climbed and fidgeted the whole
time and kept studying the hairy ear of the
man next to him. Twice, he made his mom
take him downstairs to the bathroom.

There was an organist who looked
about a hundred years old. She played
a swirling song, and people in the front
row began to move out of the church.

Ray turned around to Norma and whispered, "Is Uncle Frank still a person?"

Then they all went to the little building next door to the church for refreshments.

There were tables piled with little triangle sandwiches. Ray and Norma tried a few.

There was also a table covered with framed pictures. They were of Uncle Frank.
   Norma thought of him in the coffin, under those flowers.

Their parents seemed happy when the two of them slipped outside.

Out back, the church towered over them and it felt to Norma as though it might fall off the ground and fly away in the heat of the afternoon.

The two cousins climbed up to a little graveyard. They read the names on the stones.

They found a little pond and
looked for frogs and fish and things.

Norma found a nice feather and showed it to Ray.
Ray found a stick that he liked and showed it to Norma.

"No, no, no," said Norma in her mother's voice.
"Sticks are not toys! You'll get hurt."
Ray cried when she took his stick, but then she
wrote his name in the mud and he liked that.

Before long, Ray had to go to the
bathroom again and they went back inside.
Just before they left to go home, Norma
stopped at a huge bouquet of flowers.
In the center was a photo of
Uncle Frank, who was
smiling right at her.